Society of Friends

Rules of Discipline

and Advices of Illinois Yearly Meetings of Friends

Society of Friends

Rules of Discipline
and Advices of Illinois Yearly Meetings of Friends

ISBN/EAN: 9783337158361

Printed in Europe, USA, Canada, Australia, Japan

Cover: Foto ©Andreas Hilbeck / pixelio.de

More available books at **www.hansebooks.com**

RULES

OF

DISCIPLINE AND ADVICES

OF

ILLINOIS

YEARLY MEETING

OF

FRIENDS.

CHICAGO:

A. J. GOFF & CO., 146 CLARK STREET.

1878.

ILLINOIS YEARLY MEETING OF FRIENDS

Was established the 13th day of the Ninth month, A.D. 1875, at Clear Creek, in Putnam County, Ill., under minutes of approval from Baltimore and Indiana Yearly Meetings, by the joint action of the members of Prairie Grove Quarterly Meeting, Iowa, and Blue River Quarterly Meeting in Indiana and Illinois. It included all who were members of the Monthly Meetings then organized within the limits of these Quarters, viz. : South Western Indiana, Illinois and Iowa, and is held on the second Second-day preceding the last First-day in the Ninth month of each year.

The meeting of Ministers and Elders is to be held until otherwise directed, at 10 o'clock on the morning of the Seventh-day preceding the Yearly Meeting, and meetings for public worship at 10 o'clock A.M. and 3 o'clock P.M. on First-day, and at 10 o'clock A.M. on Fourth-day during the week of the Yearly Meeting.

INTRODUCTION.

In a measure of the power, and as we believe, under a living sense of the truth and value of the pure Gospel proclaimed by Jesus Christ, the Society of Friends was established in England about the middle of the seventeenth century, to aid in promulgating the vital truths thus taught, and increase their fruits of practical righteousness among men.

Early in the settlement of this country, meetings were established in the general order laid down by George Fox and his co-laborers, and these have gradually increased in number until seven annual gatherings or Yearly Meetings are held in the United States.

In the degree that Friends have been faithful to their profession in the years succeeding their organization, they have been concerned for the right assembling of themselves for the spiritual worship of God, and for a tender care over each other, that all may be kept true to their profession in the duties of daily life. For these purposes meetings have been established for public worship, and others for the transaction of the business of the several bodies.

As a Bond of Union we make the following statement of Faith and Principles as held by our Body.

A belief in a supreme power called God, that is primarily the cause of all things and the continual source of spiritual wisdom, light, power and truth: a universal Father, whose attributes are Love, Mercy and Justice, tenderly regarding his creation and desiring our present and future welfare.

We accept as our Distinctive Principle—a belief in the continual revelation by Christ within us, of spiritual truth and duty to individual minds that are willing to receive it, and that this revelation constitutes the bond of direct connection between God and man, and is sufficient if heeded, to save from Sin and Evil and their sure consequences.

This belief, and obedience to the revelations of the Christ within, will result in the realization of the declarations and promises contained in the Sermon on the Mount.

Righteousness consists in right doing, in obedience to the inward revelation of duty, and is manifested by unselfish love to our neighbor, dealing justly, loving mercy and walking uprightly before God and man.

Progress in Righteousness increases wisdom

and spiritual knowledge, and always tends to the happiness of man.

SIX consists in conscious wrong doing, and invariably leads to spiritual darkness and the degradation and suffering of mankind.

The testimonies springing from these beliefs, are set forth throughout our Discipline in connection with the rules of order as herein adopted by Illinois Yearly Meeting of Friends for the use and observance of the meetings and members composing it.

SCRIPTURES OF THE OLD AND NEW TESTAMENTS.

IT is affectionately recommended that Friends, especially parents and heads of families, endeavor both by precept and example to impress on the minds of the younger class, a due regard and esteem for those excellent writings, the Scriptures of the Old and New Testaments; to advise them frequently to read and meditate thereon, that the same blessed experience of the work of sanctification through the spirit of Truth, to which they clearly bear testimony, may be witnessed now as in former ages, by those who attend to its manifestations. Thus by the Divine blessing on this pious care, their youthful minds may be led into a firm belief of the Christian religion as held forth in the Scriptures of Truth.

GOSPEL MINISTRY.

——— —— —— —

BELIEVING that none can give to others what they have not themselves first received, we bear a testimony against all claim to qualification for the ministry of the Gospel of Jesus Christ, that rests for its authority upon doctrinal theological training, or upon the ordination of man, as neither of these can give a true knowledge of spiritual things or give the convicting power of the Holy Spirit, in offering divine truth to others.

We also believe the giving and receiving of a stated and continued salary as a Minister, to be contrary to the spirit and freedom of the Gospel of Jesus Christ, and therefore dangerous to the cause of true righteousness, working as a hindrance to the faithful Minister and a great temptation to such as are not thoroughly grounded upon the Rock, Christ, the spiritual Son and power of God in the soul. In saying this, we do not question the propriety and duty of supplying whatever is necessary for the fulfillment of any religious service, both to the Minister and to his or her family, where they are not able otherwise to fulfill the duty.

We believe that the Divine power alone, can qualify for Gospel ministry, and that man can only accept and acknowledge the evidence that this gift has been received through the anointing power of the Holy Spirit.

As all ability is useful when under right direction, we desire that all, including those who feel themselves called to the ministry, should carefully cultivate and use every talent they may possess, to the end that their labor may be broader and more useful, because it is clothed in the language and conceptions of a well developed mind, kept under the leadings of the spirit of Truth.

SPEECH, DEPORTMENT AND APPAREL.

As our general appearance in these matters is largely indicative of the condition of our minds, as well as helpful or otherwise to ourselves and others, as it conforms more or less to the high profession we make, we desire that our members shall be thoughtful in regard to the use of plain, kindly and honest words in their speech, avoiding extravagant phrases and formal compliments. When our minds are regulated by the spirit and purpose of the peaceable gospel taught by Jesus, we believe our speech will reflect with plainness and simplicity, the Kindness, Courtesy, Justice and Christian regard that lie back of it, in the Soul thus taught.

OUR DEPORTMENT should be in keeping with our surroundings, solid and reverent in times of worship or solemnity; calm and just during our dealings or in controversy, willing and anxious to see the right upon all sides: cheerful and kindly in the family and social relations, thoughtful of the different temperaments of individuals and differing ages, and upon all occasions avoiding hurtful conduct and maintaining a true dignity becoming our profession.

IN DRESS, decency, simplicity and utility should be observed as the essentials: neatness and good taste cultivated, and extravagance and foolish fashions avoided as being promoters of pride and vanity, and giving evidence of minds drawn aside from thoughts worthy of an intelligent, pure-minded man or woman.

WAR.

BELIEVING as we do, that the spirit of the Gospel breathes "peace on earth and good-will to men," it is the earnest concern of the Yearly Meeting, that Friends may adhere faithfully to our ancient testimony against wars and fightings, both offensive and defensive, or being concerned knowingly

in any trade or merchandise intended for such purposes, or receiving the spoils of war; neither can
we pay fines for non-performance of military
requirements.

While we recognize the need of law and order,
which in the present condition of mankind can per-
haps only be maintained by governments resting
on human authority, we believe that in the degree
that we come individually under the government of
that principle of justice and unselfish regard for the
welfare of others, that lies at the foundation of the
Christian faith, we shall render governments sustained by force, unnecessary, and build up through
self restraint, the government of Righteousness in
the earth.

As the Divine principle in the human mind
is stronger upon equal grounds than the
selfish principle, we believe that when two persons
or nations are brought face to face, the one actuated
truly by the Divine love and guided by the Divine
wisdom, and the other recognizing this fact, though
itself governed by the opposite spirit, the evil purposes will be stayed and the cause of Righteousness
progress more fully than by a conflict of arms in
anger and bitterness, even though the nearer right
of the two, should triumph. War thoroughly
demoralizes and is only better than Anarchy
opposed by helpless force.

OATHS.

But I say unto you, Swear not at all ; neither by heaven, for it is God's throne :

Nor by the earth, for it is his footstool: neither by Jerusalem ; for it is the city of the Great King.

Neither shalt thou swear by thy head, because thou canst not make one hair white or black.

But let your communications be Yea, yea ; Nay, nay ; for whatsoever is more than these cometh of evil.—*Matt.*, *5th chap., 34th, 35th, 36th and 37th verses.*

As a judicial oath rests upon the principle of calling another and superior power to witness the truth of what we declare, and is an assumption that except in this presence we would or might not tell the truth, and believing it to be contrary to the explicit injunction of Jesus, we bear a testimony against all oaths, and substitute an affirmation whenever required by law, stating that to the best of our belief and knowledge, that which we shall say will be the truth, and the truth only.

SECRET SOCIETIES.

Accepting as true, the belief that all that is good, will bear the light and should be brought to the observation of mankind generally, we earnestly advise our members to abstain from joining any association or organization whose principles are secret and, whose members are bound with oaths and required to keep hidden the general workings and designs of the body.

Such Societies, even where their purposes are good, tend to build up an exclusive brotherhood to the practical injury of that broader brotherhood taught by Jesus, and which included all mankind.

DAYS AND TIMES.

FRIENDS have always as a people avoided the use of the customary titles for the months of the year and days of the week, originally because they were mostly adopted in honor of mythical deities or idols, and because the few numerical names were no longer correct.

While there is at the present time no purpose of deification or superstitious regard in the use of the usual terms. nor any reason of this character why we should not use them, as well as the names of planets chosen in the same way, we think the simplicity and truthfulness of our numerical titles for the months and days fully justifies us in maintaining our distinct language in these cases, and therefore advise our members to adhere to the custom, as a testimony to the correct principles upon which we believe it to be founded.

Let no man, therefore judge you in meat, or in drink, or in respect of an holy day, or of the new moon, or of the Sabbath days: which are a shadow of things to come ; but the body is of Christ.—*Col. ii,* 16, 17.

As we are persuaded that no religious act can be acceptable to God, unless produced by the influence and assistance of His Holy Spirit, it is the judgment of the meeting that our members cannot consistently join with any in the observance of public fasts, feasts, or what are termed holy days, for though exterior observances of a similar kind were once authorized under the law, as shadows of things to come, yet they who come to Christ will, we believe, assuredly find that in Him all shadows end.

—

GAMING AND PLACES OF DIVERSION.

BELIEVING that wagering or giving or receiving value without returning an equivalent, is wrong in principle and destructive in practice, we bear a testimony against it in all its forms, including Lotteries, Prize packages, betting, gambling, etc., and when any of our members depart so far from the principles of honesty and right, as to participate in any of these things, early and earnest efforts should be made to convince them of their error.

'Parents and concerned friends are earnestly advised to discourage the attendance of their children and others at places of unprofitable amusement, especially such as are calculated to teach false ideas of life and duty, or to bring them into hurtful associations.

CIVIL GOVERNMENT.

FRIENDS are advised to bear themselves circumspectly toward all men, in the peaceable spirit of the Gospel ; to avoid political controversies or giving just occasion of offense to those in authority, striving to live in the daily practice of the principles of justice, truthfulness and love, and preferring our testimonies to every temporal consideration.

RIGHTS OF MEMBERSHIP.

APPLICATIONS for membership are to be made personally or in writing to the Overseers of the Monthly or Executive Meeting which the person desires to join. When the application reaches the meeting, it is to appoint a suitable committee to visit the applicant and ascertain whether his or her request rests upon sound and sufficient grounds. The committee is to report its judgment in reasonable time, and if the meeting is satisfied that membership will be profitable to the applicant and the meeting, it will enter a report to that effect and notify the person of his or her acceptance.

Any child born while its parents are in membership has a birth-right in the society, and when but one parent is a member at the time, the child can become a member upon request of one parent and consent of the other, if the meeting applied to, is satisfied to receive it.

The Overseers or a committee annually appointed in each Monthly or Executive Meeting, should extend care towards children, one of whose parents only is a member, and towards others in attendance upon our meetings who manifest a friendly interest in our principles, to see that in due season an invitation is extended to such, and the way opened for application for membership.

When members remove from the limits of their Monthly or Executive Meeting into those of another, their rights in society should be seasonably transferred; for which purpose a suitable committee should be appointed to make inquiry, and if no obstruction appears, prepare a certificate of removal, which if united with by the meeting, should be directed to the meeting nearest or most convenient to the persons.

Certificates of removal should be accepted by the meeting to which they are directed, unless there be a manifest impropriety in doing so, in which case the certificate should be returned to the meeting sending it, with due reason for the return. If the certificate be for a Minister, it should be so stated.

Certificates of any who come among us professing to be Friends, if not seasonably presented, should be inquired after.

MEMORIALS.

To commemorate the lives of the righteous is a tribute due to their memory, and may prove an incentive to the living to follow their virtues. If, therefore, any Monthly or Executive Meeting should, upon solid consideration, believe that it would be profitable to prepare a memorial concerning a deceased member, such memorial is to be sent to the proper Quarterly Meeting, where it is to be further considered, and if approved, it is to be forwarded to the Representative Committee for inspection and approbation, previous to its being laid before the Yearly Meeting, which may direct its printing with the Minutes, or otherwise, at its discretion.

It is directed that Monthly and Executive Meetings annually forward in due season, an account of the death of such members as occupied the station of Ministers, and deceased during the year.

OVERSEERS AND TREATMENT FOR DEVIATIONS.

EVERY three years or oftener, each Executive or Monthly Meeting is to appoint two or more faithful members of each sex, to be Overseers, who ought to exercise a tender and religious care over their fellow members, that if anything be manifest, that is hurtful to right principles or contrary to the harmony and good order of society, it may be seasonably attended to.

The nominations for Overseers should be made by a committee, and each name proposed be separately considered by the meeting.

If the gospel labors of the Overseers and other concerned Friends, to restore those who have violated our principles, be unavailing, the former should report the case to the Monthly or Executive Meeting without unprofitable delay. If practicable, notice should be previously given to the persons complained of, who should not sit in Meetings for discipline until restored to fellowship.

Executive and Monthly Meetings, should upon presentation of complaint against a member, enter it upon their minutes and appoint a judicious committee to extend further care in the case. This committee should give seasonable attention to the duties of its appointment.

Causes for treatment may be graded as violations of an established rule or order of the body, or of principles and testimonies involving character, and should be treated accordingly.

In cases where the departure from good conduct consists in action arising from want of matured convictions of right or from well-meant action based on incorrect principles, tender and patient care should be extended under a sense of the correcting power of the individual conscience when aroused, enlightened, and permitted time and freedom of action.

(Whenever pronouns of masculine gender are used, refer-ring to members, it is understood that they include both sexes.)

Should any member be guilty of immorality, dishonest dealing, or conduct of a criminal charac-ter, he should, when brought to a sense of the error, make written acknowledgment to that effect.

As the purpose of our labor in all cases is the restoration to sound principles, upright life and Christian fellowship, of those who have departed therefrom, it is desired that the committees in charge, shall patiently and prayerfully use all right opportunities to accomplish this end, and while diligent in this care, avoid pressing any case to an unfavorable conclusion while reasonable hope of restoration remains.

Should it finally appear in any case, that further labor or a continuance in membership would be un-profitable, a minute should be made, setting forth the cause for separation, stating that due care has been extended without avail, and that the delin-quent is in consequence released from membership; a copy of this minute should be furnished the de-linquent if desired.

When the charge against a member is for dis-honest or immoral practices, and due labor has been extended without avail, the minute of dis-membership should clearly state our testimony against the misconduct, to the end that the witness for the truth in the mind of the offender, may in future days bring to him a conviction of the justice of the meeting's action.

Differences of doctrinal belief that do not bring discord into the society, or disgrace upon its profession, are not to be causes for disciplinary treatment, as any one honestly striving after the right, and recognizing the divinity in man guiding to the truth, can, according to our faith, be safely left to this guidance while we maintain fellowship with them so far as practicable, as helpers.

When any member not under disciplinary care, nor guilty of immoral conduct, requests to resign membership with us, a committee should be appointed to visit him, and ascertain whether the desire can be properly changed and the member continued in fellowship with mutual profit, but failing in this, or where a person has become a member of another religious society, the committee should so report, and the meeting enter the request or information upon its minutes, and give a letter of release for the grounds stated in the request, if couched in proper language.

No past action of any person shall be deemed a bar to his restoration or acceptance into membership, if upon careful consideration a Monthly or Executive Meeting deems him in proper condition for membership at the time of application.

When members of a meeting reside within the limits of another Monthly or Executive Meeting and become objects of disciplinary care, the latter meeting should, upon request of the former, extend due care and forward a copy of their final judgment to the meeting to which the person belongs, and it should, if satisfied with the judgment, prepare a minute of restoration or release as the case may require.

APPEALS.

IF a member be dissatisfied with the judgment of an Executive or Monthly Meeting in a case to which he has been a party, he may give notice to the first or second meeting following the information of its action, (but none later) that he intends to appeal to the ensuing Quarterly Meeting. This notification of appeal the Meeting should record and then appoint four or more members to attend the Quarterly Meeting with copies of the minutes relative to the case, and give such explanations as may be needful.

The Quarterly Meeting is to refer the subject to a committee, (omitting the members of the meeting appealed from,) which is to carefully and diligently examine the whole proceedings in the case from its commencement, giving the applicant and the Monthly Meeting's committee each a full hearing; if the charge and offence are substantiated and the proceedings have been in accordance with our discipline, it is so to report; the Quarterly Meeting is thereupon to confirm the judgment of the Monthly or Executive Meeting, and inform the appellant of the result. If it appears that the deviation or the proof thereof is not sufficient, or that there has been irregularity in the proceedings, infringing the rights of the appellant, the committee is to report accordingly, and the judgment of the meeting appealed from should be set aside; if the ground of such reversal be irregularity of proceedings only, the Monthly or Executive Meeting is at liberty to take up the case again.

Should the appellant be dissatisfied with the decision of the Quarterly Meeting, and notify the first or second meeting following, of his intention to apply to the Yearly Meeting for a further hearing, the notice should be recorded, and four or more Friends should be appointed to attend with the minutes of both meetings in the case, and the decision of the Yearly Meeting, arrived at as in the Quarterly Meeting, shall be final.

Appellants have a right to be present in the meeting appealed to, during the appointment of the committee to judge in their cases, and objections which they may make to persons nominated, are to be duly considered and acted on by the meeting.

Appeals should be forwarded to superior meetings in the regular reports, and the appellant should be notified when to be present; also of the judgment of the meeting in the case when rendered.

QUERIES AND ANSWERS.

In order that the Yearly Meeting may be clearly informed of the state of Society, it is directed that the following Queries be read in the Monthly and Executive Meetings, deliberately considered and answers prepared, which are to be forwarded in the reports to their Quarterly Meeting next preceding the Yearly Meeting.

From the answers thus received from its Monthly and Executive branches, each Quarterly Meeting is to prepare summary answers and forward them in its report to the Yearly Meeting.

It is also directed that the first, second and eighth Queries be read in each Monthly and Executive Meeting next preceding the Second Quarterly Meeting following the Yearly Meeting, and answers thereto be prepared and forwarded to the said Quarterly Meeting.

QUERIES.

FIRST.—Are Friends diligent in the attendance of our meetings for worship and discipline? Do they avoid unbecoming behavior, and observe the hour for meeting?

SECOND.—Do Friends maintain love and fellow-ship towards each other as becomes our Christian profession? Are tale-bearing and detraction discouraged? And when differences arise are endeavors used speedily to end them?

THIRD.—Do our members observe simplicity and utility in their apparel, and avoid superfluity and vain fashions, and do they advise their children and others under their influence to the same care? Are they thoughtful to encourage plain and honest speech, and kindness, and gentle dignity in deportment, and do they guard against frivolous and pernicious literature, supplying that which is profitable and inviting in its stead, and against corrupting conversation? Do they encourage the frequent reading of the Scriptures of Truth?

FOURTH.—Are our members clear of importing, distilling, vending or using intoxicating liquors as a beverage, and do they avoid renting their property or selling their grain for such purposes? Are they thoughtful in extending a proper Temperance influence through their neighborhoods and to give due help and encouragement to the intemperate, for their reformation? Are Friends careful to discourage the use of tobacco, especially with the young, as being both useless and injurious? Do they bear watchful testimony against attending places of unprofitable diversion or of demoralizing tendencies?

FIFTH.—Are the necessities of the poor within our neighborhoods, and the circumstances of those who appear likely to need aid, inspected and relieved, so far as duty requires? As way opens are such prudently advised and assisted in obtaining such employment as they are capable of performing, and is due care taken to encourage the school education of their children?

SIXTH.—Do our members maintain a faithful testimony in favor of a free gospel ministry, resting upon divine qualification alone? Do they bear testimony against oppression, oaths, military services, clandestine trade, prize goods and lotteries?

SEVENTH.—Are Friends careful to live within the bounds of their circumstances, and to avoid involving themselves in business beyond their ability to manage? Are they just in their dealings, and punctual in complying with their engagements; and where any give reasonable grounds for fear in these respects, is due care extended to them?

EIGHTH.—When members violate any of our vital testimonies, or so act as to morally injure themselves, is due watchfulness observed to extend to them patient and Christian care, for their restoration to correct living, and unity of fellowship in the Society?

NINTH.—Are our members careful, so far as their means will allow, to give their children, and those under their care, a useful and sufficient education, under surroundings that will aid their growth in the principles of pure morality? So far as circumstances will admit, are schools established and sustained under the direction of suitable persons in membership with us?

TENTH.—Are the Queries addressed to the Quarterly, Monthly, Executive, and Preparative Meetings read and answered therein as directed?

ELEVENTH.—What Meetings have been established during the past year, and what Meetings, if any, discontinued?

It is further directed that once in each year the Preparative, Executive, and Monthly Meetings, after the reading of all the Queries and Answers, shall also have read the following Advices, that the members may consider whether they are sufficiently careful in the matters advised upon.

ADVICES.

Members are advised to observe:

Moderation in the furnishing of their houses; and, while cultivating neatness and good taste, to avoid whatever fosters vanity or causes waste of means that should be applied in useful channels.

To avoid extravagance in supplying their tables, and avoid the use of wines, brandies, or other injurious stimulants in the preparation of food; also to observe caution in the use of intoxicating liquors and opium, for medical purposes.

To avoid contracting the injurious habit of using tobacco.

To avoid being involved in political excitements, or participating in the prejudices and defamation of character so frequently indulged in during political contests; and in exercising the right of suffrage, to carefully consider our testimony against War, and neither accept any office or vote for any one under circumstances that will compromise this principle.

To keep careful watch over their temporal affairs, that others may not suffer loss through their mismanagement; also, to make wills if needful, while in health, making just distribution of their property, not forgetting the demands of benevolence when there is more than sufficient to provide for the testator's household.

To maintain Christian watchfulness over one another for the encouragement of all that is good, and for such labor with those who step into evil paths as will tend to restore them to upright life.

To extend thoughtful care towards those who meet with us in our places of public worship; to inquire after their certificates, if members of other Meetings, and to open the way for the application of rightly concerned persons not in membership in the Society.

To remember that our Christian duty is not con-

fined within our denominational fold, but that we
are responsible for all mankind as brothers and
sisters, so far as we might have influence with
them.

MEETINGS FOR WORSHIP AND DISCIPLINE.

MEETINGS for worship may be established by
Monthly or Executive Meetings when within their
respective limits, a sufficient number of interested
members reside within convenient distances of each
other.

They are to be held once or twice a week, as
seems best in the judgment of the disciplinary
meeting to which the attendants belong.

Should such a meeting be held at a place beyond
convenient reach of a Preparative, Executive, or
Monthly Meeting, it is to be known as an "Indulged Meeting," and is to be under the oversight
of the meeting establishing it, which is to report of
its care to the Quarterly Meeting preceding the
Yearly Meeting.

Executive, Monthly and Quarterly Meetings, or
the Yearly Meeting, may each annually appoint a

committee with authority to hold meetings for worship, known as Circular Meetings, when and where within their respective limits, it may appear profitable.

These committees are to report of their services as directed in the minutes of appointment.

But the hour cometh, and now is, when the true worshippers shall worship the Father in spirit and in truth: for the Father seeketh such to worship Him.—John, Chap. IV, 23.

God is a Spirit: and they that worship Him must worship Him in spirit and in truth.—John IV., 24.

Accepting these sayings of Jesus as teaching the true foundation of Divine worship, our members are earnestly advised when assembled in meetings for worship, to exclude all thoughts inconsistent with the purpose of gathering, and seek for communion with God through the influence of His power in the soul, or for profitable meditation upon subjects tending to advance righteousness in the earth.

This will bring peace and profit in the reasonable service of assembling together, and enable us to avoid drowsiness and other unseemly conduct during meeting hours.

It is also advised that our members be watchful in so arranging their temporal affairs, that these shall not interfere with regular attendance upon meetings for worship and discipline.

Meetings for business and discipline are for the transaction of such business as seems necessary for the maintenance and usefulness of the society, and members are cautioned to observe Christian dignity and forbearance, and maintain good fellowship in the transaction of all business claiming their attention, avoiding personalities or question as to motives, one of another.

OUR BUSINESS AND DISCIPLINARY MEETINGS ARE:

1st.—THE YEARLY MEETING, from which all disciplinary authority emanates. It is composed of an annual assemblage of the members of its subordinate meetings, held where and when within its limits, it by minute directs.

2nd.—THE QUARTERLY MEETINGS, each of which is composed of two or more Monthly or Executive Meetings, whose members can most conveniently assemble together. They are to be held once in three months, at such time and place within their limits as they may by minute direct.

Being subordinate to the Yearly Meeting, they are to report to it annually in writing upon all matters required by the discipline, including answers to the Queries as to the state of the Society, and each is to appoint four or more of its members to attend with the reports and represent it therein.

3d.—MONTHLY MEETINGS are composed of the members of one or more meetings for worship or Preparative meetings. These, with the Executive Meetings, are the executive bodies of the Society in all matters pertaining to its work or discipline, among its members. They are to fulfill the instructions of superior meetings in matters wherein they have authority, and maintain the established order of the general body among the members within their respective limits, each being charged with the full authority and oversight over its own members, subject to the order adopted by the Yearly Meeting.

Monthly Meetings, in accordance with their title, are to meet once a month for the consideration of such business as shall claim their attention. Every three months, at the Meeting preceding the Quarterly Meeting, they are to make a written report upon all matters required to go before the superior Meeting, and appoint two or more members to attend it, if practicable, as representatives.

4th.—EXECUTIVE MEETINGS are composed of the members of one or more Meetings for Worship or Preparative Meetings, and have the authority and general constitution of Monthly Meetings.

These meetings are to be held once in three months, at suitable times preceding the Quarterly Meeting to which they are to report. Additional meetings may be held whenever necessary, upon call of the Overseers, announced at the close of a meeting for worship.

5th.—PREPARATIVE MEETINGS are composed of the members constituting one or more Meetings of Worship. They are to receive from the Overseers, and prepare in good season for the Monthly or Executive Meeting to which they belong, whatever business needs its attention. In cases where the Monthly or Executive Meeting is composed of but one Meeting for Worship, a Preparative Meeting is unnecessary, and all business usually coming before it should go directly to the Monthly or Executive Meeting.

All the meetings for business and discipline are to keep careful record of their proceedings, the minutes being read and approved in the meeting in which the business is transacted. All certificates, minutes, or other writings issued by authority of these meetings, should be signed by their clerks on their behalf.

These meetings are each (except the Preparative Meetings) annually to appoint a committee to assist the clerks in revising the minutes of the preceding year and have them recorded in a suitable book, which is to be carefully preserved against loss or mutilation.

Representatives to superior meetings are to carry the reports from their particular meetings, and present them to the clerks of the meetings to which they are addressed, before or immediately after the reading of the opening minute. Should any such representatives, or the members of the Representative Committee, be prevented from fulfilling their appointments, they should inform the body in which the service is due, why they cannot attend, and also report to the meeting by which they were appointed.

Communications directed to the Yearly Meeting, except in the regular channel of correspondence, are to be examined by a nomination of Friends, who are to report whether the same should be read in the meeting.

Two members of each sex are to be appointed as correspondents, as often as may be deemed requisite, to forward epistles or other business to Yearly Meetings corresponding with this, and annually report their care therein.

The representatives to the Yearly Meetings are to meet at the rise of the first sitting, and agree upon and nominate to its next sitting, suitable Friends for Clerk and Assistant, who should be separately considered, and if united with, appointed to those stations.

The Yearly Meeting, and each Quarterly, Monthly and Executive Meeting should appoint and settle with its Treasurer annually.

Each Quarterly, Monthly and Executive Meeting is annually to appoint a committee, to propose Friends for Clerk, and Assistant if needed, who should be separately considered, and if approved, appointed to these services.

Each Monthly and Executive Meeting is once in three years, or oftener if necessary, to appoint a Friend to keep a record of certificates of marriage, and of removals, both issued and received; also, to record births and deaths of members, and of all burials in our grounds. The above records should be made in books suitable for the purpose.

When the Yearly, Quarterly, Monthly, or Executive Meetings shall request of those subordinate to them a copy of their proceedings in any case, the latter should readily comply, and make any change therein which the former may direct. Executive, Monthly and Quarterly Meetings when requested, should give to co-ordinate meetings, copies of such of their records as may concern them, and may at their discretion, give or refuse to their members who have had differences, copies of their minutes relative thereto.

No Quarterly Meeting is to be set up or discontinued except by the Yearly Meeting; no Monthly or Executive Meeting, except by a Quarterly Meeting; no Preparative Meeting, or Meeting for Worship, except by a Monthly or Executive Meeting.

Should a proposed new meeting be of members from more than one Monthly or Executive Meeting, these are to co-operate in establishing the new meeting, a few judicious Friends being deputed by each Monthly or Executive Meeting to attend the opening thereof. The setting up or laying down of any meeting should be reported to the next Yearly Meeting, through the usual channel.

When subjects claiming the attention of a Quarterly, Monthly, or Executive Meeting prove too difficult for settlement, they may apply by minute to their superior meeting for assistance, without naming the subject or cause of difficulty. The superior meeting is to appoint a judicious committee to sit with the meeting needing assistance, hear the cause of trouble, and give to the same, or next session of the meeting, their judgment in the case, with their reasons therefor, and if generally united with by the appealing meeting, it should be accepted and the superior meeting informed that the committee has performed the desired service.

When alterations of discipline are desired, they should be proposed in a Monthly or Executive Meeting, and if united with, forwarded in writing to the Quarterly Meeting, which, if it unites with the changes, should transmit them to the Yearly Meeting, in its regular reports. The Yearly Meeting should refer the proposed changes to a suitable committee of men and women Friends, which is to consider and report its judgment thereof, and the report is to be entered on the minutes. If any change is approved by the Yearly Meeting, it becomes a part of the Discipline, and subordinate meetings should be duly notified thereof in the usual way.

The Yearly Meeting, being the source of disciplinary authority, may, upon its own volition, make such changes as seem needful, but great care is advised against too hurried or frequent changes.

Except in cases clearly justifying it, no one ought to be appointed to any service in our meetings who is not present to accept the appointment. It is also desired that individuals and committees in nominating, and meetings in appointing any to service, shall observe a care that no other motive than the best interests of society shall cause the selection ; all who accept appointments should endeavor to fulfill the duties devolving upon them in due season and in their best ability.

Believing that male and female are one in Christ, and that the prophecy has been fulfilled wherein it is declared that " I will pour out my spirit upon all flesh ; and your sons and your daughters shall prophesy," we recognize no distinction of sex in the privileges or offices of the Society, granting the first to all equally, and appointing to the latter with a view only to individual qualification for the service needed. All our meetings for worship and business are composed of both sexes, and the business coming before any meeting may be transacted in joint session, or in separate session of men and women, as preferred; but in the latter case the two bodies should unite in judgment and constitute but one meeting in all matters affecting the body.

Should any of our members so far neglect the duty of attending our meetings as to cause fear of lukewarmness, or fail to observe good conduct therein, the Overseers and other concerned Friends should labor with such for their restoration to a sense of what is due to themselves and to the Society of which they are members.

While it is desirable, for the sake of harmonious action during seasons of supplication and prayer, that the members of each meeting should maintain, so far as practicable, the same rule of conduct, yet we prescribe no particular attitude to be observed on such occasions, requiring only that no position or action shall manifest irreverence or disapproval of the service.

During the holding of our religious meetings, care should be maintained to guard against anything tending to disorder or interruption; no public evidence of disapproval should be given during the speaking or praying of a Friend, whether a Minister or not, if the speaker is of sane mind; should any member have serious objections to what is said by any one, he should privately state them to the speaker, having first obtained the counsel and company of one or more Elders.

When our meetings are disturbed by improper communications, the Elders should take suitable opportunities with the communicant, and extend advice and counsel as may seem necessary.

GENERAL COUNSEL.

THE design of the establishment of our annual meetings being for general oversight and care of subordinate meetings, in things pertaining to the welfare of society in general, it is fervently desired that good order and concord may be maintained in them. We know that Love and Unity, founded upon Christian principles, are promotive of truth and righteousness among ourselves, and we believe that when manifested in us, they will have their influence for good upon those around us. We therefore fervently desire that He who hath to the present day preserved us a people greatly blessed, will graciously be pleased to animate us with a zealous concern that love may predominate and concord and peace prevail in every department of our religious body. May all our meetings be held with due solemnity, as in the immediate presence of the Head of the Church, and the reverence becoming the worship of Almighty God, be conspicuous in our assemblies.

May the aged among us be examples of every Christian virtue, evincing by the calmness of their evening, that the labor of their day has not been lost. May the middle aged not faint in their places in the heat of the day, but with encouragement for the aged and the young, firmly support and exalt the precious principles and testimonies of Divine Truth.

May the beloved youth bend cheerfully under the forming hand of Holy Goodness, each standing in his allotment, that the harmony of the building may be preserved and we truly be as temples in which the Lord of Hosts can make manifest His power and His goodness.

MEETINGS FOR MINISTERS AND ELDERS.

Once in three years or oftener, if circumstances require, Executive or Monthly Meetings are to appoint a joint committee of men and women, which on solid deliberation, is to propose two or more upright and judicious members of each sex, to fill the station of Elders. The names proposed should be separately and weightily considered by the meeting. If the nominations are approved, they are to be members of the meetings of Ministers and Elders, and information should be given to the Preparative Meeting of that body, of the appointment. The above triennial appointments are to be considered as a release to those who are in the station of Elders, though such are not ineligible for re-appointment. When Elders remove from one Meeting to another they are to receive certificates as members only.

The Ministers and Elders of a Monthly or Executive Meeting, or of more than one if the Quarterly Meeting advises it, are to meet once in three months, and compose a Preparative Meeting of Ministers and Elders; all these Preparative Meetings, within the limits of a Quarterly Meeting are to meet once in three months, and compose a Quarterly Meeting of Ministers and Elders; and all these Quarterly Meetings within the compass of the Yearly Meeting are to meet annually, and compose a Yearly Meeting of Ministers and Elders. The particular time and place of holding these meetings are subject to the meetings for discipline to which they are severally attached.

Meetings for Ministers and Elders are not to interfere with the disciplinary affairs of the society.

As much depends on the conduct and example of Ministers and Elders, these meetings have been established among them for the purpose of examining whether they are all preserved in exemplary conduct answerable to their stations, and where advice and caution may be administered for the help and strength one of another, as may appear necessary; with this view the following queries are to be read and answered in them.

First, by each Preparative Meeting, in which explicit answers are to be given thereto in writing, and forwarded in its reports to the Quarterly Meeting of Ministers and Elders by a suitable number of representatives; the queries are to be read by the latter in connection with the answers from their Preparative Meetings, of which correct summaries should be minuted; those made at the meeting next preceding the Yearly Meeting of Ministers and Elders, should be included in the reports thereto and forwarded by a suitable number of representatives.

In the Yearly Meeting of Ministers and Elders the queries should be read with the answers from its Quarterly Meetings, and summaries thereof made and recorded.

QUERIES FOR MINISTERS AND ELDERS.

1.—ARE Ministers and Elders diligent in the attendance of Meetings for worship and discipline so far as ability is afforded, and concerned to encourage their families to that religious duty?

2.—Do Ministers, in the exercise of their gifts give evidence of divine qualification?

3.—Do Ministers and Elders maintain Christian fellowship one with another, and with the meetings to which they belong. Do they manifest a religious concern for the advancement of truth, and the proper observance of our good order?

4.—Are Ministers and Elders good examples in uprightness and moderation of conduct, and are they careful to instruct their families in the principles and testimonies of our religious society? ·

It is also desired that the following advices be deliberately read in each subordinate select meeting, at least once in the year.

ADVICES TO MINISTERS AND ELDERS.

1.—That Ministers in their testimonies, be cautious in using unnecessary preambles, and of asserting too positively a divine impulse, the baptising power of truth accompanying their words being the true evidence.

2.—That all read the Scriptures of Truth frequently and be careful when quoting from them to do so correctly.

3.—That Ministers guard against prolonging their sermons beyond the lively and clear presentation of truth in their minds, and against the unnecessary addition of remarks, after they have once spoken.

4.—That Ministers use great caution in presenting doctrinal statements as being essential to religious life, and avoid raising questions on those points, which they cannot clearly answer or leave in profitable shape.

5.—That they be careful not to hurt their service by singing intonation, affectation, or gestures which do not comport with Christian gravity.

6.—That the Elders remember that they are set, in part, as helpers and judges of a true gospel ministry, and should carefully fulfill these duties of their station, by entering into travail of spirit with ministers in their services and extending to them at suitable seasons, due counsel either of caution, advice or approval, as their conduct and service may show needful.

7.—That as Elders, more fully grown in Christian knowledge and experience, they should be watchful for the uprising of spiritual life in the membership and extend encouragement and help to the young and faltering, seeking for divine wisdom to nurture and admonish these aright.

8.—That Ministers and Elders dwell in that unselfish concern and travail of spirit which gives ability to labor successfully in developing the spiritual life in themselves and others, being examples in conversation, in charity, in purity of life and faithfulness in Christian duties.

When a Friend has appeared in the Ministry and the Preparative Meeting of Ministers and Elders is united in proposing to the Monthly or Executive Meeting, that he be recorded as a Minister, it is to inform the Quarterly Meeting of Ministers and Elders thereof; if the latter concur, then the former should propose the consideration of the subject to the Monthly or Executive Meeting, and if it on weighty deliberation, should unite in approving the ministry of the Friend, it is to inform the Preparative, and it the Quarterly Meeting of Ministers and Elders thereof, when the person becomes a member of the select meetings.

When a Minister apprehends that it is his religious duty to travel in the ministry beyond the limits of his Monthly or Executive Meeting, he should lay the subject before it for its counsel and judgment. If the meeting believes the minister is rightly called, it should give a minute of unity and concurrence.

No Friend is to travel as a Minister or appoint meetings beyond the limits of his local meeting, unless previously recorded by a Monthly or Executive Meeting. It is not intended hereby to debar any Friend from accompanying a Recorded Minister within the limits of his Quarterly Meeting, or in a more extended journey, if the concurrence of the Monthly or Executive Meeting be obtained.

When any one has appeared acceptably in the ministry, giving reasonable assurance of having a gift in that direction, but has not been recorded, the meeting to which the person belongs may grant liberty to such person to appoint occasional meetings within its limits, whenever, in its judgment, it is right to do so.

Should a Minister have a concern to make an extensive visit among those not of our society, or a general visit in another Yearly Meeting, the concurrence of the Quarterly Meeting is to be obtained and indorsed on the Monthly or Executive Meeting's certificate, unless from some peculiar circumstances, the Monthly or Executive Meeting should conclude that too great inconvenience would result, when this should be stated in the certificate given.

When a Minister has a concern to make a religious visit to Europe, or to other foreign parts, as the clearest evidence of the duty should be manifest, the concern, together with the certificates of the Monthly or Executive and Quarterly Meetings, is to be laid before the Yearly Meeting, and, if there approved, a final certificate should be given.

As the performance of religious visits to families, under right direction, has proved useful and instructive, it is advised for the encouragement of Ministers, that those who have a concern to make a general visit of this kind even in the meeting to which they belong, should have the concurrence of the meeting, and a minute, if the concern extends to the families of another meeting.

Should Ministers, when remote from home on appointments of the Yearly Meeting, have a concern to appoint a few meetings, they should obtain the approbation of the committee in company, or of such other Friends as may be convenient, before proceeding therein.

Believing that occasions may arise in which a Minister absent from home may feel a right concern and qualification for religious service under conditions that prevent the obtaining of a minute or the counsel of Friends, it is provided that any recorded Minister in good standing may under such conditions, appoint a meeting or fulfill the conceived duty while it is fresh and clear, but in such cases, a report of the service should be made to the meeting of which he is a member, at an early date.

In granting visiting certificates to Ministers, the character and limits of the service should be stated in the certificate, which ought to be returned in due season after the time for the performance of the duty specified, has passed.

When Friends traveling, present visiting certificates from their respective meetings, they should be read, and if no obstruction appears, a minute should be made of their attendance and of such religious services as may be approved.

Should Ministers or Elders, by unfaithfulness or otherwise, lose their usefulness so as to render it advisable that they should be released from their stations, a timely and tender care should be extended by individuals, and if necessary, by the Preparative Meeting of Ministers and Elders of which they are members; if they cannot be thus restored to usefulness, the case should be laid before the Quarterly Meeting of Ministers and Elders, and if, in its judgment, a release is advisable, it should so report to the Preparative Meeting of

Ministers and Elders, and the latter inform the Executive or Monthly Meeting to which the persons belong, which may then remove them from their stations.

REPRESENTATIVE COMMITTEE.

In order that the Yearly Meeting may be properly represented between its annual sessions, it is directed that each Quarterly Meeting forward once in three years, in its reports to the Yearly Meeting, the names of three suitable members of each sex, who, with twenty-one members of each sex, appointed by the Yearly Meeting, are to constitute for three years, a Representative Committee, which is to hold its meetings at such time and place as the Yearly Meeting may direct. The committee is privileged to meet on its own adjournment, or to call a special meeting whenever eight members shall judge it necessary.

It is to be governed by the following rules:

1.—It shall keep record of all its proceedings, and report to each Yearly Meeting the minutes of the preceding year.

2.—Twenty members shall constitute a quorum capable of transacting business.

3.—It is to notify the Yearly or Quarterly Meetings when vacancies occur in its membership, which are to be filled by appointment from the meeting that previously appointed to the places vacant.

4.—The committee is not to adopt any article of faith or discipline.

The services confided to the committee are:

1.—In general, to represent the Yearly Meeting between its annual gatherings and act on its behalf in cases where the interests or reputation of our religious society may render it necessary.

2.—To have the oversight and inspection of all manuscripts proposed to be printed in the name of the society, relative to our religious principles or testimonies, and to advise or discourage their publication as may seem best; it may also publish such writings as it approves and draw on the Treasurer of the Yearly Meeting to defray the expense incurred in these or any other services.

3.—To inspect and maintain titles to land or estates belonging to any of our meetings, and to advise or attend to the appropriation of charitable legacies and donations.

4.—To receive from Quarterly Meetings such memorials concerning deceased Friends as shall be forwarded, and give them the necessary inspection

and correction, that they may be laid before the
Yearly Meeting.

5.—To extend such advice and assistance to persons under suffering for our testimonies as their
cases may require, and if necessary, apply to the
authorities in their behalf.

6.—The committee may correspond, as occasion
requires, with like representative bodies of the other
Yearly Meetings.

7.—All Friends with visiting minutes, and members of other Representative committees are entitled
to sit with this committee, and other concerned persons may do so by its consent.

8.—Any member desiring to publish a book,
pamphlet, or paper upon the religious principles
or profession of the society, should lay the subject
before the Representative Committee for its counsel and advice, or be well guarded in causing it to
appear upon each copy printed, that it is done upon
the responsibility of the writer alone, and not by
permission or authority of the society. The Representative Committee and the Yearly Meeting,
alone have the authority to publish official statements of our principles, and their publications should
always have the imprint of their authority.

MARRIAGES.

MARRIAGE being an ordinance affecting all the relations of life, it is affectionately advised that, before any propose to enter therein, they do humbly ask the counsel of the Lord; and if they have a clear evidence of Divine approval, that they acquaint their parents or guardians with their intentions, and give due heed to their deliberate advice, so that they may be preserved from the dangerous bias of uncertain affection and from the bitter fruit of improper marriages.

Our members are earnestly advised to proceed in the beautiful order given in our Discipline when taking upon themselves these solemn obligations, and when contemplating marriage with those not in membership with us, they are affectionately advised to consider and sustain the important testimony of this people in favor of a free gospel ministry, and avoid calling in the aid of a salaried minister upon such occasions.

It is the settled conviction of Friends that the marriage of our members with those who do not hold our principles and testimonies, is very frequently productive of evil results to the parents and their offspring; and it is earnestly advised

that parents and concerned Friends take early opportunities to discourage such connections. If,
however, marriages occur among us contrary to
our order, the members are to be visited thereafter
by the Overseers, and if they have violated any of
our testimonies, endeavors are to be used to restore
them to a sense of their error.

Marriages of persons sooner than one year after
the death of a husband or wife, or between first
cousins, or the children of half-brothers or sisters,
are not allowed among us.

Marriage being a solemn covenant for life, and
the fulfillment of its obligations so essential to the
welfare of family life and the maintenance of
society itself, we cannot recognize divorces and re-
marriages while both parties are living.

In extreme cases of persistent cruelty, rendering
life insecure, or the fulfillment of marriage vows by
the injured party improper, legal separation without divorce is permitted.

A divorce and re-marriage contrary to this rule is
not however, to be considered a perpetual bar to
membership, if the meeting to which such person
may apply is, after solid consideration, satisfied that
the membership will be profitable to the person and
the meeting.

When any of our members are rightly engaged

to enter the marriage covenant, the following fair and honorable order is to be observed:

The parties proposing marriage with each other, if belonging to the same Monthly or Executive Meeting, are to communicate their intentions to the Overseers one week or more before the holding of said meeting. The Overseers are to make all necessary inquiries as to the clearness of the parties from other similar engagements. If the woman be a widow with children, they are to see that these have their legal rights properly secured.

Having seasonably fulfilled these duties, the Overseers are to forward the request with a report of the result of their inquiries to the next meeting, which if satisfied that all needful care has been taken, shall set the parties at liberty to accomplish their marriage according to the order of the Society, at such time and place as may seem proper.

The Overseers, or a suitable committee appointed by the meeting, should attend the marriage, see that good order is observed, and that the certificate is duly signed by the contracting parties and a suf ficient number of other friends as witnesses; they should also place the certificate in the hands of the meeting Recorder for early record. In cases where State laws require, the certificates should be duly copied upon the public records and the original returned to the persons married.

Should the man be a member of another meeting than the one to which the woman belongs, he is to produce a certificate from the Overseers of his meeting, setting forth his membership in society, and that inquiries have been made and nothing found to prevent his entering into marriage relations as proposed, when the meeting should proceed in the usual course.

Should one or both of the parties to a proposed marriage under the order and care of society, not be in membership, it should be so stated in the application, and all subsequent proceedings be the same as in marriage of members.

The form of request presented to the Overseers should be as follows :

To ——— *Meeting of the Society of Friends :*
DEAR FRIENDS—With Divine permission and your approbation, we intend marriage with each other.   Signed,   A—— B——.
                                          C—— D——.

A marriage having been authorized, and the company gathered for its accomplishment, it is advised that a season of quiet solemnity be observed, after which the parties to the marriage are to rise in the presence of the assembly, and taking each other by the hand, the man is to audibly declare as follows :

"FRIENDS—In the Divine presence and before this assembly, I take —— —— to be my wife, promising to be to her a faithful and affectionate husband until death shall separate us," when she in like manner shall declare that she takes the said —— —— to be her husband, promising to be to him "a faithful and affectionate wife until death shall separate us."

They are then to sign the marriage certificate, the woman according to custom taking the family name of her husband, and a suitable person previously designated by the attending committee, should read it, including their signatures, before the assembled company. The certificate should afterwards be signed by the members of the committee, and a portion at least, of the persons present as witnesses.

The form of marriage certificate is as follows:

WHEREAS, —— —— (man's name), of —— (town), in the county of ——, and State of ——, son of —— —— and —— ——, his wife, of ——, in the county of ——, in the State of ——, and —— —— (woman's name), daughter of —— —— and —— ——, his wife, of ——, in the county of ——, and State of ——, having informed —— Meeting of the Society of Friends, that they intend marriage with each other, and no obstruction appearing, (consent of parents or guardians being given, if the parties are minors,) their proposal of marriage was allowed by said meeting.

This is to certify, that in the accomplishment of their marriage, this —— day of —— month, in the year ——, the said —— —— (man's name) and —— —— (woman's name) appeared at (here state the meeting place or residence where the marriage is accomplished), and in the presence of a committee of said meeting and other witnesses, the said —— —— (man's name) took the said —— —— (woman's name) by the hand and declared that he took her to be his wife, promising to be to her a faithful and affectionate husband until death should separate them ; and she the said —— —— did in like manner declare that she took him the said —— —— to be her husband, promising to be to him a faithful and affectionate wife until death should separate them, they did then and there sign their names to this certificate, she in accordance with custom assuming the family name of her husband.

(Man's name)   A. B.

(Woman's name) C. B.

And we being present at the solemnization of said marriage, have subscribed our names as witnesses thereto.

————————————   ————————

————————————————————————

————————————————————————

It is affectionately advised that the parties to a

marriage, their parents and others concerned, take
care that moderation at the entertainments following the marriage be observed, and that no reproach
arise to any of our testimonies. If anything to
the contrary be observed, proper admonition
should be privately and speedily given, and if the
advice be not heeded, the case should be reported
to the meeting.

BIRTHS, DEATHS AND FUNERALS.

Each Monthly and Executive Meeting is annually
to appoint a committee to collect an account of the
births and deaths within its membership, which is
to be handed to the Recorder for record ; also to
have charge of the meeting's burial grounds, and see
that they are properly inclosed and kept in decent
order. The committee is to see that our plain and solemn order is observed at the funerals of all members who are buried in our grounds.

Should any person not a member make request
upon reasonable grounds for permission to bury in
our cemeteries, and be willing to forego the erec-
tion of costly or extravagant memorial stones, in
harmony with our testimony in this respect, per-

mission may be granted at the discretion of the committee in charge of funerals. In the spirit of religious toleration no objections should be made to the performance of any quiet, orderly burial service preferred by the friends of the deceased.

It is advised that our members avoid all extravagance or vain display in the conduct of funerals, manifesting by their plain apparel and solid deportment, their sympathy with the solemnity of the occasion; also, that no monuments or extravagant memorial stones be erected within our burial grounds. This is not intended to prohibit any modest and reasonable headstone or tablet to mark the resting place of the deceased.

The following form of record is proposed, as being both simple and explicit:

BIRTHS.

Names of Children.	When Born.	Names of Parents.	Their Residence.	Occasional Notes.

DEATHS.

Names of Deceased.	Date of Death.	Age	When Buried.	Late residence.	Occasional Notes.

PARENTS AND CHILDREN.

ALTHOUGH spiritual life does not descend by lineal inheritance, helpful or hindering temperaments do, and we therefore urge upon parents to guard and restrain with great care their own tendencies to whatever is evil or excessive in their nature, and to encourage and increase whatever is good or deficient, not only as a duty to themselves, but as a help to their offspring, who will inherit their parents' temperaments in greater or less degree. As children are given to their care, parents should be faithful in watching over them for their moral growth, moulding their character in gentleness and wisdom, remembering their proper craving after things suited to their ages. They should endeavor to inculcate sound principles and lead the children to the self-application of these principles to their daily needs, rather than to furnish them conclusions resting in the wisdom of another. It is especially desired that they be restrained from pernicious reading and conversation, and their need for that which is instructive and cheerful be supplied, and that they be taught the nobility and beauty of right doing, as well as the duty. Let parents endeavor to educate their children in a reverent respect for goodness, purity, and virtue, and thus may we be twice blessed in our efforts, once in our own lives and again in the lives of our children.

SCHOOLS.

As knowledge gives increased qualification for usefulness, it becomes us as a people to encourage a thorough and liberal education for all, and provide for the instruction of our children and those within our influence, in whatever is useful and within the limit of their capacity and our ability. As children need moral as well as intellectual education, and are very much influenced in this respect by their surroundings during the impressible period of youth when their characters are forming, great care should be observed to see that these are helpful and good. So far as practicable it is desirable that they should attend schools under the care of teachers holding views consistent with our testimonies, and who are concerned for their right presentation to their pupils. Were our members sufficiently impressed with the value of such care, it is not doubted that many schools would be established and maintained among us, and our children generally, receive a guarded education. We earnestly recommend the thoughtful consideration of this subject to our members in their several neighborhoods.

TRADE.

UNLESS the love of justice, mercy and truth be manifested in our dealings with men, we can have no claim to practical religion. Friends are therefore earnestly advised to avoid all hazardous enterprises, especially when the means of others may be involved, and to be cautious as to becoming surety for any; also not to choose such callings as may bring reproach upon any of our testimonies, but rather to make choice of such vocations as are useful, and be diligent therein; to keep their accounts accurately, and inspect them often, that they may know whether they are living within their means; thus reserving to themselves the ability to be not only just to all, but helpful to the unfortunate.

If any have doubts of their ability to fulfill their engagements, or to pay their just debts, they should immediately consult some judicious Friends, and if they advise it, make a full exhibit to their creditors of their assets and liabilities, and as they may direct, use the former to discharge the latter, by assignment or otherwise, but without partiality. Friends are not to avoid the payment of their just debts by any legal privileges or transfer of property, but to make pro rata payments as they may become able.

If any of our members neglect the above limitations in their business pursuits, or give rise to fears that they are doing so, they should be labored with, and if their conduct is at variance with our advice or reproachful to society, prompt and judicious care should be extended to them.

The assignees of such as have failed, should use diligence in the collection and speedy distribution of the assets among the creditors.

Friends are advised to be careful not to receive collections or bequests from such as have not paid their just debts. Also to consider well the ground before indorsing or becoming surety for others.

ARBITRATIONS.

Should differences arise between members of our society about their temporal affairs, the party thinking he has reason for complaint, having endeavored by quiet and reasonable efforts, to obtain justice, without avail, should ask one or more judicious Friends to join their endeavors. to have the matter justly and speedily settled ; or if the distance between the parties be too great, the complainant should propose the same course by writing, and failing in that, should empower some Friend to pursue the course above indicated on his behalf.

Should the case appear to be a plain one, or a debt against which no reasonable objection is made by the debtor, the Friends are to advise the party complained of to make satisfaction without arbitration or further delay ; but should unsettled differences in accounts, or reasonable cause for dispute appear, which cannot be settled between the parties themselves, they are to advise them to submit the case to arbitration. If either party refuse to do this, such refusal is to be reported to the Executive or Monthly Meeting in which the proceedings are to be reviewed, and if the above gospel order has not been duly observed, the case should be referred to a committee without being minuted; but if the proceedings in the case are approved, the meeting should appoint a committee to labor with the unjust party, in disciplinary order.

If either of the parties be dissatisfied with the award, and it be evident that arbitrators have erred materially in their proceedings or judgment, the meeting may apply to the Quarterly Meeting for assistance, as directed in difficult cases, and should it clearly appear that there is cause for dissatisfaction, a re-hearing is to be granted, and other arbitrators chosen, whose decision is to be final.

When parties conclude to submit their differences to arbitration, they are to choose a suitable number of Friends for that purpose, and enter into a written agreement to abide by their decision. Subject to the foregoing order, the arbitrators chosen should promptly appoint a time and place and attend to the business without unnecessary delay, giving the parties and their witnesses a full and fair hearing in the presence of each other, and within reasonable time make the award.

It is advised that Friends in the ministry be not chosen as arbitrators in any case.

When the foregoing proceedings, by causing delay, would evidently endanger the rights of, or subject the complainant to unjust loss, which might be avoided by a more direct legal process, Monthly or

Executive Meetings may hold such excused as apply to the law from such necessity; but they are cautioned to conduct themselves toward each other with such kindness and moderation as will be a becoming testimony, even in court, that only the nature of the case, and our station under the laws of the land, bring any of us there.

When like differences occur between persons one of whom is a member and the other not, if the person not a member is willing to adopt this method by arbitration, the case should be proceeded with, while the non-member remains a consenting party.

If any member arrests or sues another at law, in disregard of the foregoing rules, he should be labored with in due order, as for other improper conduct.

PROPERTY AND CASH FUND.

QUARTERLY, Monthly and Executive Meetings are directed to make timely and careful inspection into the situation of the titles of meeting houses, burial grounds, and other estates which have been vested in trustees, for the use and benefit of said meetings, so that, if it should appear needful, upon the death of any such trustees, or from other cause, due and seasonable care may be taken to appoint others to the trust, that future difficulties and the risk of being deprived of such estates may be avoided.

And it is further directed that Quarterly, Monthly and Executive Meetings respectively, as the case may require, keep exact records of all such trusts and conveyances; also that a clear and regular account be kept by each respective meeting, of the place where and the person with whom its papers, minutes, and records, belonging to our religious society, are, from time to time deposited, due care being taken to lodge them with suitable members.

1.—A cash fund having, by experience, been found useful for the exigencies of the society, it is directed that such a fund be maintained by an occasional collection from each Quarter, in the proportions which may, from time to time, be determined by the Yearly Meeting; and that it be placed in the hands of the Treasurer appointed by the Yearly Meeting, and be subject to be drawn out by its direction, or by the Representative Committee, as required.

2.—Quarterly, Monthly and Executive Meetings are also directed to raise and keep a fund, to be used for such purposes as their respective wants may render necessary.

APPENDIX.

A BRIEF account of the origin of some of the names commonly used. for the months in the year. and for the days of the week :—

1.—January was so called from Janus. an ancient king of Italy. whom heathenish superstition had deified : to whom a temple was built. and this month dedicated

2.—February was so called from Februa. a word denoting purgation by sacrifices : it being usual in this month for the priests of the heathen god Pan to offer sacrifices and perform certain rites. conducing. as was supposed. to the cleansing or purgation of the people.

3. — March was so denominated from Mars. feigned to be the god of war. whom Romulus. founder of the Roman Empire. pretended was his father.

4.—April is generally supposed to derive its name from the Greek appellation of Venus. an imaginary goddess. worshiped by the Romans.

5. — May is said to have been so called from Maia. the mother of Mercury. another of the pretended

heathen deities, to whom, in this month, they paid their devotions.

6.—June is said to have taken its name from Juno, one of the supposed goddesses of the heathen.

7.—July, so called from Julius Cæsar, one of the Roman Emperors, who gave his name to this month, which before was called Quintilius, or the fifth.

8. — August, so named in honor of Augustus Cæsar, another of the Roman Emperors. This month before was called Sextilis, or the Sixth.

The other four months, namely, September, October, November, and December, still retain their numerical Latin names, which, according to the last regulation of the calendar, are improperly applied. From the continued use of them hitherto, as well as from the practice of the Jews before the Babylonish captivity, it seems highly probable that the method of distinguishing the months by their numerical order only, was the most ancient, as it is the most plain, simple, and rational.

As the idolatrous Romans thus gave names to several of the months, in honor of their pretended deities, so the like idolatry, prevailing among the Saxons, induced them to call the days of the week by the names of the idol which, on that day, they peculiarly worshiped.

Hence, the first day of the week they called Sunday, from their customary adoration of the sun on that day.

The second day of the week they called Monday, from their usual custom of worshiping the moon on that day.

The third day of the week they named Tuesday, in honor of one of their idols called Tuisco.

The fourth day of the week was called Wednesday, from the appellation of Woden, another of their idols.

The fifth day of the week was called Thursday, from the name of an idol called Thor, to whom they paid their devotions on that day.

The sixth day of the week was termed Friday, from the name of Freya, an imaginary goddess by them worshiped.

The seventh day was called Saturday, from Seator, worshiped by them; or from Saturn, an imaginary deity of the Romans.

ERRATA.

On page 11, bottom line, omit "opposed by helpless force," and substitute "with violence."

INDEX.